by Rebecca J. Allen

COLE CHAMPION IS NOT SUPER

illustrations by
Courtney Huddleston

Book design by Jake Slavik
Illustrations by Courtney Huddleston

Published in the United States by Jolly Fish Press, an imprint of North Star Editions, Inc.

First Edition
First Printing, 2022

Library of Congress Cataloging-in-Publication Data (pending)
978-1-63163-588-5 (paperback)
978-1-63163-587-8 (hardcover)

Jolly Fish Press
North Star Editions, Inc.
2297 Waters Drive
Mendota Heights, MN 55120
www.jollyfishpress.com

Printed in the United States of America

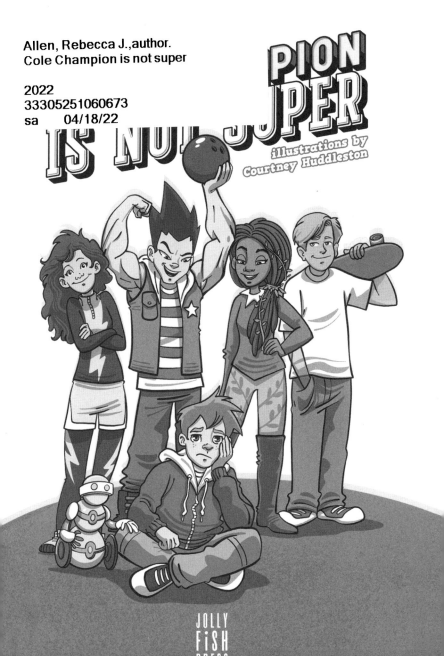

PION
SUPER
IS NOT SUPER

illustrations by
Courtney Huddleston

JOLLY
FiSH
PRESS
Mendota Heights, Minnesota

Chapter One

Honor, Endurance, Resolve, Optimism Junior High

When you're the only "normal" at a school for the superpowered, you've got two options for surviving the school day with the least trouble possible. Option one: You trail HERO Junior's principal (aka, Mom) into the school to avoid being challenged by Supers flexing their muscles. Then you stay within a ten-foot radius of a teacher or administrator at all times. This option is foolproof. Just ignore the supersized serving of humiliation you feel for being so helpless you need the protection of adults.

Option two: you go on your own and hope for the best.

And by *you*, I mean *me*.

As Mom turns the minivan into the entrance of HERO Junior High, my shoulders instinctively tense up. I'm not ready for another day of this "excellent educational opportunity," as she calls it. But that won't get me out of going to class.

The sky is blue with just a few puffy clouds. The Superhero Alliance flag in front of the school flutters in a light breeze. It's the type of day that makes future superheroes dream of saving humankind, then being invited to the White House for a photo shoot and brunch with the president. It makes *me* wish I went to any school other than this one.

Today is going to be different, I tell myself. Today is the day I stop using Mom as a bodyguard. Today is the day I brave the Supers on my own.

Mom turns off the engine and reaches for her bag in the front passenger seat. Then she looks back at me. "Ready?"

On the seat next to me, my bot, Sidekick, lets out a beep with an ascending pitch. He's trying to be encouraging. But I'm not feeling it.

I remind myself that if I were at Middletown Junior High, the public school my best friend goes to, I'd hang outside until the warning bell rang. I want to be able to do that here too. So, I shoot Mom a huge, fake-cheery smile and say, "Sidekick and I want to get some fresh air before class."

Mom's sky-blue eyes peer deep into mine, like she's looking inside my skull at the activity of my brain to see if I'm hiding anything.

I mean this literally. With her X-ray vision, she *can* see my brain. But even with her power, she can't read my thoughts.

"Good idea." Her eyes now sparkle. I recognize the warning sign. She wants to wrap her arms around me in a big, sappy hug. But she knows hugs are off-limits—a *zillion times* off-limits within sight of classmates. Fortunately, she just nods, steps out of the car, and strides toward the school entrance, her high-heeled super boots clicking against the blacktop.

Great. Now I'm committed. I press back into my seat, savoring the last moments of safety within the steel frame of our minivan, and gather my courage. Then I turn to Sidekick. "We better get our butts in motion before any more Supers show up."

The bot swivels his head to the side, his eyes dropping to where his butt would be if he were shaped more like a human and less like a snow-man—three stacked, white balls, one for his head, one for his chest, and one with two wheels attached at the sides so he can move.

Sidekick started out as a standard robot kit Dad got me for my birthday because he knows I love anything STEM-related—that is, Science, Technology, Engineering, and Math related. But thanks to some coding upgrades Dad and I worked on and some hardware upgrades made in the well-equipped auto garage my best friend's mom owns, Sidekick's much more than a standard bot now. Sometimes, his artificial intelligence makes him seem almost human.

I heft Sidekick onto the blacktop and sling my

backpack over one shoulder. The front steps are an ideal spot to enjoy the last few minutes before class—right in the sun, and near the school entrance if we need to make a quick escape. But the walk to the steps is treacherous. Lots of Supers show up early for pre-class workouts. These are more about showing off their powers to the rest of the student body than about building muscle.

So, my mission: reach the front doors without being spotted by enemy agents. I scan my surroundings for threats.

Behind me on the running track, Bolt stirs up a small cyclone as she runs a couple warm-up laps. She's tall and lean. Her tan skin and black-and-gold tracksuit flash by as she picks up speed.

"I'm outta here," she calls to warn whoever's around. I cover my ears just in time to deaden the deafening clap as she takes off for a quick lap of the tri-state area, breaking the sound barrier as she accelerates.

My jaw dropped the first time I saw Bolt take off. Now it's just part of the new normal of going to a school full of Supers.

Next to the running track is a skate park complete with a quarter-pipe, a half-pipe, and a bowl where Supers can practice ollies and 360-degree spins. How exactly will skateboarding help Supers catch villains or save humankind from peril? Beats me, but this school has every perk imaginable. Ghost uses the skate park to practice turning invisible in mid-action. He also uses it to show off his tricks in case Bolt's watching during her warm-up.

Now Ghost zooms up one side of the ramp, vanishing as his skateboard flips through the air and reappearing when it hits the concrete again.

His skin and hair are almost as colorless as the white metal of Sidekick's frame. He zooms toward the opposite ramp, in his zone. He's paying no attention to me.

In the open field past the skate park and in front of the greenhouse is Thorn, a Super with plant powers. She spends her time before school nudging the grass to grow into new and ever-more-complex hedge mazes other Supers can use to practice tracking villains. Her brown hands wave gently over the strands of grass in front of her, which sway as they grow as high as her shoulders, then higher still, twisting together to create a solid wall.

Thorn's not so bad. She's given me a small smile once or twice. It almost seems like she doesn't fit in at HERO Junior High any more than I do, though I can't figure out why. She's got one of the coolest powers in the seventh grade. I'd love to find out how it works—maybe she speeds up plants' ability to make their own food through photosynthesis?—but I'm too shy to ask.

I look beyond Thorn to the hill where my nemesis, Boulder, usually spends his mornings. He likes to roll this huge hunk of rock up the hill to build his muscles. He could do it a zillion times a day and not get bored, which makes me think his head is full of rocks too.

Today, though, the hill is clear. Which means Mission Don't Get Spotted is a go!

"Lock doors," I whisper to Sidekick. My shoulders

bunch up again when the minivan beeps at Sidekick's Bluetooth command.

I scan my surroundings one last time. Thorn's eyes are on her grass. Ghost's skateboard does a spin in midair. Bolt is nowhere to be seen. She's probably rounded New Jersey by now, but I've still got a few seconds while she laps Connecticut.

There are no Supers between me and the school building.

I pull up my hood, stuff my hands in the pockets, and tiptoe through the narrow space between the two rows of parked cars to avoid notice. Sidekick glides silently behind me.

I pass three cars. No visible threats.

I pick up my pace. *Only two cars left . . .*

The front tires of the last car fly two feet into the air, then drop with a *thud*, almost landing on my foot.

"GAH!" I jump back in shock, then look around like it wasn't me who made that high-pitched shriek. (It totally was.)

And who steps out but Boulder, looking buff in his blue denim vest with its white-star patch, red-and-white striped shirt, and chunky boots. The All-American outfit shows off bulky biceps no normal seventh grader would ever have. Boulder's light-tan skin glistens with a sheen of sweat, and his straight, jet-black hair is gelled up, defying the laws of gravity. "Cole, just the guy I wanted to see."

Mission Don't Get Spotted status update: complete and total failure.

Also—Boulder almost crushed my right sneaker, as well as every bone inside it. But does he apologize? No. Typical.

"Morning, Boulder," I mumble. Sidekick beeps a hello as well. I start walking again—thanking the universe that I still have two working feet—when Boulder's hand lands on my shoulder, stopping me.

"Watch me pick up the front of this car with one hand, Cole." He pushes down on my shoulder—*ouch!*—as he demonstrates his car-lifting skill.

"Awesome," I grunt under the strain on my shoulder. "The best. Watch where you put that car down."

Boulder laughs. "Don't worry. I've got this." He puts a second hand on the car's bumper and screws up his face as he lifts it all the way over his head. He's clenching his teeth so hard they might crumble into bits and rain down on the blacktop. There's a shriek of grinding metal as the back bumper hits the pavement. Some teacher's going to be annoyed when they get back to their car this afternoon.

But I'm free, so I turn toward the front doors again. I don't even make it one step before I hear a *thud* and Boulder's hand is back on my shoulder, heavier than before.

"That's why *I* deserve to be here at HERO Junior High," he says. "But what about you, Cole? Show us what you've got."

Us? My stomach does a flip-flop.

I look around and see Bolt is back. Darn! Why is Connecticut such a small state? Ghost is visible again and standing nearby, his skate helmet propped against one hip. Even Thorn is walking our way.

Sidekick beeps his low "uh-oh" tone.

Four Supers ready to prove I'm not cut out for HERO Junior High. My worst nightmare. Why didn't I just slink into school safely with Mom?

I have no dreams of a photo op and brunch with the president. I'd just like to fit in at this school. But I guess that's too much to ask.

Chapter Two

The Challenge

"**F**ree your mind, Cole, and you'll free your power," Ghost says, his voice as otherworldly as the far-off look in his eyes.

Even when Ghost is visible, you could imagine invisibility was his superpower. The white, metallic sheen of his fitted T-shirt almost matches his complexion. His eyes are mismatched, one a pale blue and the other brown like mine. And he exudes this fairy vibe, like his home is a circle of mushrooms in some untouched part of the forest rather than a house down the street.

"Yeah," Bolt agrees. "Your mom's a Super. Maybe your power just needs a nudge."

I wish nudging my power had any chance of working, but I've been trying to nudge it for as long as I can remember. Most Supers' powers appear before they can even walk. If mine hasn't come out by now, their encouragement isn't going to turn me into a Super right this millisecond. It's more likely to jinx me.

"I bet you've got super strength deep within you." Boulder pinches my bicep and frowns. "Really, *really* deep within you. Try to lift the car two-handed. Not everyone can do it with one hand, like me." He waves at the bumper in front of me.

I stare at him in disbelief.

"If you feel Super, you'll be Super," he insists.

I want to tell him and Ghost their motivational quotes belong on silly posters of rainbows and mountain scenery. I also want to crawl under the car and hide rather than humiliate myself by trying to be Super and failing. But Boulder is in half my classes. He's not going to stop bullying me just because I tell him I'm not Super. I've tried that before. He'll only be satisfied when I prove I have some power, something other than a superhero mom, that qualifies me for a spot in this school. Or when I transfer to another school.

Anyway, I'm tired of Boulder's challenges. My muscles are nothing super, but I've got a zillion super-cool STEM facts in my head.

Thinking of STEM gives me an idea. A great idea. One that will have that bumper off the ground in no time.

"Hold on!" I tell Boulder, and "Unlock the car!" I call to Sidekick as I run for the back of Mom's minivan. We keep a spare tire and a hydraulic jack there.

Mom would not approve of me using the jack on my own, but Dad showed me how to use it when we had a flat tire last month. Also, I'm not planning on doing anything more dangerous than what Boulder was already doing.

I lower the jack to the ground and raise its long lever so I can roll it to Boulder and the car I'm supposed to lift. "Get ready to witness the power of simple machines—a lever and fulcrum."

"A lever and what now?" Boulder frowns.

A crease forms between Bolt's eyebrows, but Thorn shoots me a small smile that does strange things to my stomach. The vine twisted into her long braids grows out toward the jack, as if reaching to touch it, but she tucks the vine gently behind her ear. As I kneel down and slide the jack into place under the car's back end, I direct my explanation to her.

"This long bar on the car jack is basically a lever, a simple machine that makes work easier by multiplying human force. Inside the jack is a fulcrum, a small support the lever rests on. When I push down on this side of the lever, the other side moves up. It's like a seesaw." The jack is a bit more complex than this. It also uses hydraulic fluid and pistons, but I focus on explaining only the lever and fulcrum. Too much STEM knowledge at once might make Boulder's brain explode.

I push down on the lever a couple times, lifting the car inches off the ground. Boulder grunts and crosses his arms over his chest, looking unimpressed. But Thorn looks interested, and Sidekick encourages me with three sharp beeps.

"The fulcrum is closer to the car than to my hand. The long length of the lever where I'm

applying force multiplies my power, so even though
I don't have super strength like Boulder, I can lift
something as heavy as a car. I'll need to apply force
to this lever a bunch of times, but the STEM power
of this simple machine will allow me to lift the car

and meet Boulder's challenge. I can even do it one-handed!"

As I talk, I keep moving the lever up and down, up and down. It's not impossible, like lifting the car bare-handed would be for me, but it's not super easy either. I need to put my body weight into moving it. I'm getting good and sweaty, and I'm breathing hard. But I keep talking. It's my only shot at convincing Boulder that I don't have to be Super to have something to contribute at this school.

After a minute, the car's bumper is about a foot and a half off the ground, almost as high as Boulder got it one-handed. I met his challenge, just using STEM rather than a superpower.

Thorn claps, and I give her a small bow.

But Boulder snorts. "You cheated. You were supposed to use your power, not a tool."

"Why is that cheating?" I ask. "You wanted me to lift the car, and I did."

"But what if you didn't have that jack," Boulder says. "You'd have no power."

"Being Super isn't what's important," I say. "Having a solution to the problem is. What if a little kid was standing at the bottom of that hill you roll a boulder up every morning and you dropped it?" I wave at the hill beyond the hedge maze. Boulder has worn the grass off a path straight up the hill with his training. "Your super strength couldn't stop the rock once it started tumbling. Only Bolt is fast enough to be able to get the kid to safety."

Bolt straightens and props her fists on her hips. Her chin's raised like she's posing for reporters writing a story about her great prospects as a superhero. She probably thinks my point is that her superpower is better than Boulder's. These Supers—always arguing about whose power is the greatest. As if being a Super isn't awesome enough, they all want to be the *most-Super* Super.

Boulder puffs out his chest and flexes his biceps. "I'd never drop that rock. I work out ten times every day, sometimes more. Before I'm in high school, I'll be ready to challenge Captain Republic in a competition of strength."

"Oh no, I don't think so." Thorn's index finger twitches back and forth, and the vine threaded through her braids mimics the motion. "You can't stop the rock once it's rolling. It would be ahead of you and you've got super strength, not super speed. Cole's right. You wouldn't be able to save the kid."

This starts a full-on argument, pitting Thorn against the three other Supers. Part of me wants to stay and watch Thorn defend me, but I also know this is my chance to escape. Boulder and the others are arguing so much, they've completely forgotten about me and the car I lifted off the ground.

I release the jack, carefully lowering the car, and put the tool back in Mom's minivan. "Come on, Sidekick." The bot follows as I trudge into the school, feeling dejected.

I'll never fit in at HERO Junior High.

Chapter Three

The Power of STEM

I tug open the door to Mr. Slumber's science classroom. Sidekick rolls to his spot next to the table I sit at on the far side of the room. No one's here yet, not even Mr. Slumber.

"Hey, Al." I salute Einstein, who stares at me from a poster on the wall. He's my idol, a theoretical physics superhero.

I pull my binder out of my backpack and slide the bag underneath the table. Even though school only started a couple weeks ago, the binder's already stuffed because science is my favorite class. But the answer to how to fit in at HERO Junior High isn't in there. If levers and fulcrums didn't impress the Supers, no STEM topic will.

Sidekick gets my attention with a four-note tune that mimics the rise and fall of my best friend Mireya's name.

"You're right, buddy, let's call her."

He puts the call through via his Bluetooth connection with my smartphone. His eyes swivel in his head, switching from visual-input mode to projection mode, and Mireya's head and shoulders appear in the space in front of Sidekick. Her brown skin, warm smile, and out-of-control curls are so familiar. My humiliation from Boulder's challenge fades.

The back of Mireya's bus seat is in Sidekick's 3D image. So is the face of the boy in the seat behind her as he photobombs our call. He pulls a funny face and adds bunny ears to Mireya's head.

"Still on the bus?" I'm great at stating the obvious.

"Fifteen minutes early for science class again?" Mireya says back. Yeah, we're predictable.

Mireya tilts her head and leans in toward the camera on her phone. "You look like you've already been hit by a Boulder this morning."

I sigh, tugging on the strings of my hoodie. I want more than ever to go to Middletown Junior

High with the one person who gets me the best. I tell her about Boulder's challenge, Thorn's defense, and how I used a jack to lift a car. "I explained how it worked and everything."

Mireya nods. "Lever and fulcrum."

"But Boulder said it didn't count because I used a tool, not a superpower." I throw my hands up. "Every day at this school, I feel like a loser. The Supers are constant reminders that I lost the hereditary lottery. I had a one-in-four chance of getting Mom's recessive genes for blue eyes and a superpower. Instead, I ended up with Dad's dominant genes for brown eyes and freckles."

Mireya lifts an eyebrow. "And his brain for science and engineering."

When I'm with Mireya and we're designing and building stuff in an unused bay of her mom's auto repair shop, Dad's science and engineering genes feel like enough. More than enough. Awesome, even. But not here.

"I wish there were do-overs in genetics like there are in video games. I could reroll my chromosomes and get better genetic stats."

Mireya's eyes bug out like she's horrified. "Don't wish that! STEM is full of awesome powers, even if Boulder doesn't appreciate them. Someday that rockhead is going to need your STEM knowledge. Then he'll be sorry for all his challenges."

Sidekick lets out his high-pitched, peppy beep in agreement.

"And anyway"—Mireya's expression turns mischievous—"it sounds like *someone* there is starting to appreciate you."

"What? Who?" I ask.

"Thorn? You've been mentioning her more and more lately."

"I don't know what you're talking about."

"No?" Mireya doesn't look convinced. "Isn't she the one who you said grew the nicest Venus flytrap you've ever seen? And you really want to talk photosynthesis with her?"

"Uh . . ." My mind races. "Oh no! The connection's failing. I can't hear anything—are you talking? And the video is fizzing out—" I frantically gesture to Sidekick to end the call. The last thing I hear is Mireya's laughter.

Sidekick's eyes swivel back to visual-input mode. He somehow manages to look disapproving.

"Don't look at me like that," I say. "She'll get to tease me all she wants tonight." Middletown's science fair is coming up. I'm heading to Mireya's after school to help brainstorm project ideas with her. "Though there's *nothing* to tease me about," I continue. "Obviously. Because there's *nothing* there. Like a—like a *black hole* amount of nothing." Except black holes are actually filled with a tremendous amount of stuff. . . . Shoot! I need a distraction.

I open my binder and start a list of possible topics for Mireya's science fair project. Last year, she filled clear tubs with different types of soil—sandy, pebble-filled, and dense—then squeezed a thick, magma-like substance in from the tubs' bottoms to show how the earth's surface is affected by magma rising. This year's project has to be even better. She could grow plants that demonstrate dominant and recessive genetic traits, or design her own solar oven, or . . .

Chapter
Four

Mr. Slumber's Surprise Experiment

I'm so deep in thought about my project ideas that it takes me a while to realize the classroom is filling up.

Boulder and Bolt are still arguing when they stomp in. But their seats are on opposite sides of the classroom, so all they can do is glare at a distance. Good thing they don't have laser vision. Ghost glides silently to his seat in the row behind Bolt. Thorn doesn't take this class. She and the other plant powers have an alternate science class with a strong biology focus.

Mr. Slumber arrives just before the bell rings.

"Are you ready for a great day of science, class? Today, we'll begin our new section on kinetic and potential energy with an experiment." Mr. Slumber rubs his hands together like this experiment is going to be the best thing ever, but half the students in the room are still talking, not even paying attention.

Mr. Slumber's superpower is putting people to sleep. He used to be a full-time hero, with his phone connected to Central, where the Superhero Alliance dispatches heroes to save humankind from peril. But now he just puts future heroes to sleep with his science lectures.

Not me, though. A science experiment sounds awesome to me. I wonder what it is, because our classroom looks the same as it always does. There are no notes on the whiteboard and no setup for an experiment on our tables.

The chatter in the room finally quiets as Mr. Slumber heads not to the whiteboard, but to three bowling balls resting against the back wall of the room. "I need volunteers. Grab these balls, then follow me outside. Bring your notebooks too."

"Don't worry, Mr. Slumber," Boulder says, jumping up from his table. "I can take all three, easy."

He trips over Sidekick in his rush, and Sidekick lets out a high-pitched beep of horror as he falls onto his side, his wheels spinning uselessly in midair.

"Careful!" I say, but my voice is too low and Boulder is too focused on showing off his muscles to notice. I set Sidekick upright. The bot lets out a low whir of thanks.

Ghost and the rest of the class follow Mr. Slumber outside, but Bolt strides to the back of the room to help with the bowling balls.

"I've got this." Boulder has a ball in each hand. He tries to use the one in his right hand to push the third ball into the crook of his left arm and fails. All three balls drop with a *thunk* on the floor.

Grinning, Bolt grabs a ball.

Boulder moves to block her path to the door. "I said I'd get them all." Annoyance is clear in his tone.

Part of me is glad I'm not the only one Boulder bosses around. Another part knows these two will be here arguing until the end of the period if I don't do something. I want to see this energy experiment, so I head for the ball that rolled nearest me.

"Chill, dude." Bolt leans in, getting into Boulder's face. "It doesn't take super strength to lift a bowling ball, and I can move faster."

Boulder stands taller, trying to look intimidating. His face reddens with frustration. "I can lift all three. I'll get them outside faster than you. With your puny arms, you can only carry one at a time."

"I can carry two," Bolt says, reaching for a

second ball, but Boulder blocks her. "And even if I couldn't, I can make three trips outside and back faster than you can pick three balls off the floor."

Boulder gives Bolt the stink eye. "Is that right?"

Bolt's tracksuit flashes as she zooms around Boulder, finally grabbing the second ball from the floor.

"Hey!" Boulder gets low, spreading his arms wide to try and block her in.

Meanwhile, I've already got the third bowling ball in hand. I grab my science binder as Sidekick and I head out the door.

"Hey!" Boulder yells after me. "You're not even Super. Give me that ball!"

"If I feel Super, I'll be Super," I call cheerily over my shoulder, smug that the strongest Super in school can't carry a single bowling ball.

Chapter Five

Cole Champion's Hypothesis

As Sidekick and I head outside, I feel a sharp gust of air blow by—Bolt racing to the experiment. I hurry after her, hoping Boulder won't catch up. It's not the bright, cheery day it was earlier. Clouds hide the sun. The Superhero Alliance flag cracks in a gust of wind as if warning of trouble to come. But what trouble could come from a cool STEM experiment?

Sidekick and I pass the greenhouse where Thorn

and a few other plant-power Supers are turning baby vines into a lush jungle that winds up the glass walls. Sidekick calls out a friendly beep and I wave—because it's the *polite* thing to do, not for any other reason. Thorn smiles, and a bud on the plant she's standing next to blooms into an enormous purple flower.

Very pretty, I think. The flower, that is.

I think back to the argument with Boulder and the other Supers in the parking lot this morning. I shouldn't have left Thorn there alone. I should have stayed and defended STEM knowledge with her. I need to thank her later for helping me.

I walk by the hedge maze. A Super almost slams into me as she sprints out of the nearest entrance, yelling, "Olly olly oxen free!" What that means literally, I'm not sure, but when a PE class plays Track the Villain, it means she's won and everyone else can come out and organize for the next round of the game.

Sure enough, three other Supers come sprinting out of the maze. The first jogs left to miss me, the second jogs right, and the third slams right into me, sending my bowling ball into the air and me onto my butt.

"Uh-oh," Sidekick squeaks, his visual sensors pointing up toward the sky.

My eyes follow, and it feels like time slows down. The bowling ball is about to drop right onto him, shattering his head and every circuit in his round little frame. Every muscle in my body tenses—just like when Ms. Adrenaline, the social studies teacher, caught me sleeping in class and jolted me awake with a zap of her power—yet I can't make myself move in time to avoid this disaster.

I see a flash of moving limbs, and suddenly a Super is there, handing the bowling ball to me with a "sorry, dude."

It's Slo-mo, the best guy to have around when you've got a problem you can't move fast enough to fix. He can finish a math test in the time it takes the rest of us to write our names on the top of our papers when he's showing off. He must have slowed his perception of time so he could swipe the ball out of midair before it hit Sidekick. Now that the crisis is averted, he's returned to normal speed.

"Whoo." I sigh with relief. Sidekick lets out a beep in the same pitch.

I haul myself to my feet and nod at the Super who just endangered, then saved, my bot's head in the span of a single second. Brushing dirt off my butt, I pass the maze to find my science class.

Mr. Slumber and my classmates are gathered

around three long wooden tracks. Each track is about ten yards long and the width of a bowling ball. They each start at Mr. Slumber's height, then swoop down and up along different paths.

Bolt has placed her bowling balls at the start of two of the tracks, so I heft mine onto the third track. Then I open my binder and do my best to draw the path of each track.

The closest track swoops down almost to ground level, then swoops up and down a smaller bump, before ending back up almost as high as it started. The second track has a shallower first hill. After a second hill, it ends with a line of grooves the bowling ball will have to roll over. This track ends at about half the height of where it started. The last track has a couple big swoops but finishes close to the ground. All tracks start at the same height.

I start forming a hypothesis, which is my prediction of which track will allow its ball to roll fastest. The steep incline at the end of track one will slow down its ball a lot. The grooves on track two will cause more friction, slowing down the ball more than the smooth surfaces on the other tracks. The third track starts high and ends low. Even though it has a couple big swoops in the middle, it's my pick to be the fastest. All the tracks start at the same height, which means the same potential energy. But track three ends with the lowest potential energy, meaning the ball will maintain more kinetic energy and speed until the end.

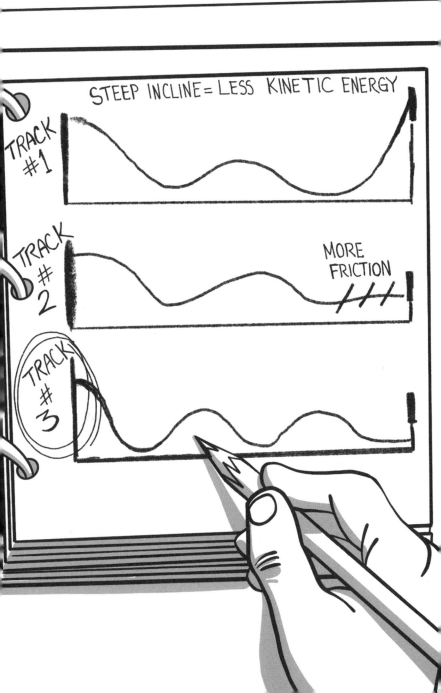

I can't help but smirk. I've picked the winning track without needing to see any ball move an inch. Boulder—who is just now arriving—shoots me and then Bolt the stink eye.

Mr. Slumber starts his lecture. "Potential energy is energy stored by an object's position, like a bowling ball at the top of an incline. Kinetic energy is the energy of an object in motion."

He tips the ball on track one off its starting position. It swoops down the track and up, down and up, before hitting the barrier at the end of the track.

"The first high hill gives the ball lots of potential energy," Mr. Slumber continues. "That potential energy is converted to kinetic energy as the ball rolls down the hill. The ball loses some of its kinetic energy and its speed as it climbs the next hill, because the energy is changing back into potential energy. But since that hill isn't as high as the first one, the ball will make it over the hill and pick up kinetic energy again as it rolls down the far side."

I know all this already. My dad explained it to me this summer at an amusement park as we waited in line for a roller coaster. I add the idea to my list of potential science fair projects for Mireya—she could build a miniature roller coaster demonstrating kinetic and potential energy. It could even have a 360-degree loop.

"What does any of this matter?" Ghost mutters nearby.

"It matters a lot to skateboarding," I say absently.

"The speed you pick up as you roll down the ramp. How you slow down and eventually stop in midair after zooming up a ramp. Though, of course, that's gravity playing a role too."

Ghost looks at me in surprise.

Mr. Slumber claps his hands. "So, the question I pose to the class is: Which track will allow its ball to reach the end first?"

Boulder puffs up his chest. "The ball I push will travel fastest. No value to super speed on this task." He glances at Bolt.

"Super strength is not the point either," Mr. Slumber tells him. "All the balls will start at the same time with the same initial force. There are levers on each track to control for this."

Boulder scowls. "This is a school for Supers. What's the point if you can't use super strength to make the ball roll faster?"

"The point is to know how the laws of physics work before we break them," Mr. Slumber says. The teacher turns to me. "Cole, what is your prediction for which track's ball will finish fastest?"

"Number three," I say without hesitation. "They all have the same potential energy at the start, but track three has the lowest ending point, so its ball won't lose as much kinetic energy, or speed, by rolling up a slope at the end. It also has no grooves to create additional friction and slow the ball down."

"I like your reasoning." Mr. Slumber looks around at the class. "Any other predictions?"

"I predict I can learn plenty about kinetic energy and get a workout at the same time if I roll that boulder to the top of this hill." Boulder starts toward where his favorite rock waits for his next workout.

Potential energy, I think. Kinetic energy is the energy of movement. The rock will only have that when it rolls *down* the hill. But it will gain potential energy from Boulder shoving it up the hill. I don't say this out loud though. Boulder is in a mood.

"I'll let you know when I've got it to the top and I'm ready for your predictions about how much faster it will go than your bowling balls," Boulder calls over his shoulder.

"You'd be better served by staying here and participating in the class discussion, Boulder,"

Mr. Slumber says. But he doesn't really argue. The teacher can probably sense that Boulder needs to work off some steam.

Boulder reaches the hunk of stone. It's as tall as his chest. He stretches his arms wide, prepping for his workout. Then he starts shoving the rock up the hill.

Good. That will keep the rockhead occupied so the rest of us can learn something.

Chapter Six

A More Dangerous Hypothesis

"**I** need one student at the start of each track to launch a ball," says Mr. Slumber. "Cole, take track one. We don't want you to get overexcited and help the ball on track three." Ghost is assigned track three, and another Super takes track two.

Three other students are positioned at the end of each track. Mr. Slumber hands them stopwatches. "Start the timers when I say 'go' and the balls are released. Stop as soon as the ball on your track hits the barrier at the end. We'll record the times, then repeat the experiment three times to make sure we have accurate results."

Everyone gets into position.

"Ready?" Mr. Slumber asks. When we all nod, he says, "Three, two, one. Go!"

I press the lever, which tips the ball down track one. The balls are neck and neck until near the end where track one's slope becomes much steeper than track three's and track two has those grooves. The ball on track three clicks the barrier an instant before the other two.

"Yes! I knew it!" I thrust a fist into the air. "The ball on track three won."

This is my jam. There is something so satisfying

about understanding the laws of physics and being able to make accurate predictions about how things will work. The world can feel chaotic, especially when Dad's watching the news and villains are endangering humankind or politicians can't agree on anything. Science makes me feel like I can count on the world working the way it should.

"Excellent," Mr. Slumber says. "Cole's hypothesis was correct. But this is science, my friends. We must be thorough in testing our hypotheses. Let's run the experiment again to make sure we made no mistakes."

A classmate named Scorch hands me the bowling ball for track one. I nearly drop it because it's hot in a way that couldn't have come from friction. "Yowch!"

"Sorry!" the Super says with raised hands that glow red.

I sigh and set the ball in its starting position. While I wait for the others to get ready, I glance over at Boulder. I'm surprised to see he's only three-quarters of the way up the hill.

I look down at Sidekick. "That rockhead is sweating like he was when he lifted the car over his head this morning."

The bot sounds his "uh-oh."

I lower my voice so only Sidekick can hear me. "Why 'uh-oh'? It's good to see he actually has to work hard at something."

I put my finger on the lever to release the ball and wait for Mr. Slumber's signal. Sidekick lets out another warning beep. I look back at Boulder just as the teacher says, "Go!"

I'm so surprised to see Boulder's muscle-bound arms trembling, I almost miss flipping my lever on time. My eyes don't follow the bowling balls. Instead, they track the Super straining on the hill. He's not moving. Then, he falls to one knee. The rock rolls back, looming over him.

I'm getting some major future-superhero-in-trouble vibes.

"Boulder, are you okay?" I shout. The kids recording the balls' times miss their results as they also turn to Boulder.

"Fine," he says, but he doesn't sound fine. His voice is shaky. "I just need to rest a minute."

"You need to rest holding two hundred pounds of rock up on an incline?" I ask, because that just does not compute.

"Three hundred pounds," Boulder calls back. His second knee drops to the ground.

This is *not* good.

Sidekick mimics the wail of an ambulance's siren. It's his emergency sound. But that can't be right. Is it even possible for super strength to fail? My heart must think so because it's pounding double time.

"Boulder, you've overdone your workouts today," Mr. Slumber calls up to him. "Start back down the hill." The calm in the teacher's voice might fool Boulder, but the rest of us can see Mr. Slumber's hands are clenched into tight fists. The vein in his temple bulges.

Boulder's arms are almost straight up now. He's straining to keep the rock from rolling backward onto him.

I form another hypothesis, and it's not a good one. Boulder will not be able to push that boulder to the flat surface at the top of the hill. He's not going to be able to get it back down the hill either. Boulder's favorite boulder has a whole lot of potential energy in its position, and it's about to convert that to a whole lot of kinetic energy as it tumbles back down straight toward us.

Another shudder hits Boulder, this time shaking his entire body.

"Argh!" He sucks in a deep breath and furrows his brow as if redoubling his effort to hold the rock. "Don't worry. I got this."

But unlike when he was lifting cars this morning, he doesn't look like he's got it.

A dark cloud passes over the sun, and a chill runs down my spine. "We've gotta get out of here!" I yell.

"I agree with Cole's assessment," Mr. Slumber says. "Class, leave your things and head into the building."

Everyone stays frozen. They all stare at him with wide eyes.

"We'll be all right," Bolt says. "Boulder's a Super."

"Supers aren't invincible, Bolt," Mr. Slumber says. "Remember last year when Captain Republic was rescuing earthquake survivors from collapsed buildings for a week? He got a call to apprehend Destructa, and she ended up getting away because he'd overtaxed his muscles. Superheroes are powerful, but they can still wear themselves out. This is especially true for heroes-in-training."

Boulder lets out a low groan.

"Bolt, get Mrs. Iceberg!" Mr. Slumber says. "She can create an ice wall to hold that stone in place until Boulder recovers enough to move it."

"Got it. I'm outta here," Bolt says. Notebooks, timers, and Mr. Slumber's clipboard clatter to the grass as everyone covers their ears. Bolt takes off in a flash.

I don't think Mr. Slumber's plan is going to work. Bolt will have reached Mrs. Iceberg's classroom already. But Mrs. Iceberg moves at glacial speed, and that rock isn't going to wait for her. We need a plan we can set in motion *now*.

"Move it, the rest of you!" Mr. Slumber bellows at the class.

The others charge for the school, but I stand there tugging on my hoodie strings. My feet are quaking in my sneakers, but I can't move. I know how potential and kinetic energy work. Even with the science class clear of the rock's path, we've still got two problems.

Behind me, the maze is full of Supers playing Track the Villain. There's no way we can make sure everyone's clear of it in time. Beyond the maze, the greenhouse is in the boulder's path too. The walls are covered in jungle greenery by now. Thorn and the other plant-power Supers have no clue that a giant boulder is about to throttle down the hill,

crushing the tracks for the science experiment,
the maze, and the greenhouse all in one long path
of destruction.

Chapter Seven

Cole Champion Faces Super Danger

Sweat streams down Boulder's face. He lets out another groan. "I could be wrong about being able to hold this, Mr. Slumber. You'd better get clear too."

"I'm sticking with you, Boulder," the teacher calls out. Then he turns to me and says in a low voice, "But you should get a move on, Cole. I don't want to be responsible for getting Principal Champion's son crushed by that rock."

"I can't go. I need to find some way of stopping its kinetic energy so it doesn't demolish the maze and the greenhouse," I say.

Mr. Slumber's brown skin turns a shade paler, like he was only thinking about the problem in front of him, not the additional problems behind him.

I think back to Slo-mo and the other kids in the maze. Slo-mo can slow time, but only *his* perception of time. And even if he could slow time for Boulder, it would just leave Boulder holding up that rock for longer.

Who were the other Supers in the maze? I try to remember, though I know it's no good. There are a zillion different powers Supers can have. But only one person at HERO Junior High has super strength, and that's Boulder. Even with a school full of Supers, not one of them can help us out of this crisis.

I look around for something we can use to prop the rock in place. Thorn's maze of grass won't stop the boulder. It would hardly slow it down. A couple cars from the parking lot could stop it, though they'd get bashed up in the process. But the boulder's path won't take it to the parking lot, which is off to the left.

The cars get me thinking. There's something else to the side of the rock's path. Something that could easily absorb the kinetic energy of a three-hundred-pound boulder. It would save the maze and the greenhouse from getting smashed and prevent Mr. Slumber or some other teacher from having to walk home this afternoon.

The skate park.

I spring into action, running to the space between Boulder and the skate ramp. "Sidekick, with me," I call out. My little bot sounds an optimistic beep like he knows what I'm thinking and approves.

Pointing one arm up the hill toward Boulder and the other arm down the hill toward the quarter-pipe, I make sure I have the angle right. "If the boulder comes this way," I call to Mr. Slumber, "it will roll up the slope of the quarter-pipe, into the half-pipe, and then up and into the skating bowl. In the bowl, it could roll around and around until friction finally stops it. Then everyone will be safe."

Mr. Slumber nods grimly. "But that's a big *if*."

Sidekick checks the angle. He lets out two high beeps to let me know I'm right.

"Boulder!" I shout, and he glances over his shoulder. He looks nothing like the cocky Super who scoffed at me for lifting a car with a jack this morning. He's got huge sweat stains under his pits, and his gravity-defying hair is plastered to his forehead. He looks like a Super who's about to see his career defending everything that is right and good get crushed before it ever starts, as a result of unintentionally killing his classmates.

What does a Super who can't save people do with his life? Maybe teach science at HERO Junior High. That would be fine as a career for me, but torture for Boulder. His whole life is wrapped up in his super strength and in becoming the world's greatest superhero.

Boulder looks so wiped that I worry he won't be able to pull off what I'm about to ask, even though, normally, it would be a breeze for him.

"Look where I'm standing," I tell him. "You need to move the boulder over a bit so it rolls toward me and the skate park. This way, everyone in the maze and the greenhouse will be safe."

"Easy for you to say. I don't have any strength left to move this thing. I'm not sure I can even keep it where it is." The rock slides a bit, pushing Boulder a couple inches farther down the hill. The huge stone looms over him like he might just be the first of several people it flattens.

No. We definitely can't wait for Mrs. Iceberg. We need to act *now*.

My nerves are taut. I tug my hoodie strings back and forth so hard the cord hurts the back of my neck. I use Boulder's own corny motivational words to encourage him. "If you feel Super, you'll be Super. You lifted a car over your head this morning. You just have to move that rock over a couple feet. Then you won't have to keep holding it."

Boulder's arms tremble, and I know he'd love to let that huge hunk of rock go. But he doesn't move. "What if you're wrong, Cole? You're no Super. If I let this roll down the hill and someone gets hurt, I'm the one responsible."

That is a huge responsibility. Boulder needs to avoid hitting the maze and the greenhouse, but he also can't overcorrect or he'll send the boulder out into the road. It could hit a car or a cyclist moving down the street.

"You're right," I tell him. "I'm no Super. So doesn't that make it *more* impressive that I lifted the back end of a car? I have super-STEM knowledge, Boulder. Trust me."

The look on Boulder's face says he does not want to trust me. But his quaking muscles mean he has no choice.

Boulder takes a sharp inhale and shouts out,

"Aaaaargh!" as he shoves the rock in my direction. His body strains, and his face turns bright red as he puts every ounce of his super strength into moving the boulder over just a couple feet.

Then he repositions himself to keep the rock from tumbling. "Here?"

I check the angle. Sidekick checks too. "Uh-oh," the bot chimes.

"Close," I tell Boulder. "You're almost there. Just a few more inches." Every muscle in my body tenses, and I desperately hope the Super's exhausted muscles are up to the task.

Boulder groans as he presses against the rock again. "Here?"

I check the hill between him and the skate park for any bumps or dips that might set the boulder on the wrong path. It's clear.

"Yes, that's it!" I shout. "Let it go!"

Boulder dives to the side, face-planting to the ground in exhaustion. The rock careens down the hill, converting its potential energy into kinetic energy, and picks up speed fast.

With Sidekick and me directly in its path.

Chapter Eight

Cole Champion's STEM Superpower

"**M**ove, Sidekick!"

I dive out of the way, then look back to make sure my bot is clear.

He's not. My heart jumps into my throat and sticks there so I can hardly breathe.

One of the little bot's wheels is caught in a rut. His other wheel spins as he tries to gain enough momentum to pull himself out, but he just ends up spinning round in a circle, trapped in the boulder's path. "Uh-oh, uh-oh, uh-oh," Sidekick beeps at a pitch so high I didn't even know he could hit it.

The ground beneath us trembles. The rock's almost on top of him.

A long, leafy vine darts out to wrap itself around the bot's short, metallic arm. It yanks hard, sending Sidekick flying through the air toward me. He hits the ground at my side with a *thunk* that makes my heart lurch just as the boulder thunders past us, missing both of us by inches.

I collapse to the ground in relief, panting, and try to get my heart rate back under control. I squeeze the bot's arm as the rock flies up the quarter-pipe and hangs in the air for a fraction of a second before crashing down into the half-pipe.

It rolls up the other side, catching air again before it hits the bowl with an ear-splitting *smack*. Then it circles a moment, dissipating its kinetic energy, just as I said it would.

"Woot!" Mr. Slumber screams. "You did it!"

"Whoa." Boulder pushes himself slowly up from the ground. He finger-combs his hair until it's in place, defying gravity again. "I can't believe I held that rock as long as I did."

I would roll my eyes at him, but I'm too relieved. I lie back on the grass. The cloud blocking the sun finally clears, turning the day bright and warm again in an instant. A huge smile tugs at my lips.

I hear cheering behind me. Bolt's back. Thorn and the other kids from the greenhouse and the hedge maze are with her. They're all clapping. I think for a second they believe it's Bolt who saved them, or maybe Boulder. Then I realize they're all staring at me.

It hits me: I saved them with my STEM knowledge. For the second time today, I feel like it's as good as their superpowers. Even better, since Boulder's power failed but STEM powers never will.

Someone else walks up behind the students. I meet the piercing-blue, unamused eyes of Principal Champion. And she is *not* clapping.

"Cole Percival Champion," Mom says, stalking toward me.

"Oh no," I say.

"Uh-oh," Sidekick agrees.

It's never good when my ridiculous middle name comes out of Mom's mouth. I made her promise to never, *ever* use that name at school, but she's staring at me like I've lost my mind. She plants her fists on her hips. Her face is growing even redder than Boulder's was a minute ago.

"Just what do you think you are doing?" Mom's voice is strained. "I did not enroll you at HERO Junior High so you could endanger yourself by charging into the path of falling boulders. I thought you had more common sense than that, Cole. Leave saving the day to the Supers!"

Her disappointment in me stings. But instead of feeling small like I did when the Supers challenged me this morning, I feel a fire heat up deep in my gut. Before I can stop myself, I blurt, "You're wrong!"

Mom looks surprised that I'm talking back, and I'm surprised too. But I keep going.

"I have a power as good as any superpower. I have STEM knowledge, and that's what saved the maze, the greenhouse, and the people inside them. I did it as well as any Super could have."

What am I saying? This is my chance to convince Mom I don't belong at HERO Junior High and get her to enroll me at Middletown Junior High with Mireya instead. Why am I defending my place here?

Mom sucks in a deep breath, but before she can get any words out, Boulder cuts in.

"Cole's right. I didn't believe him this morning

when he said he could lift a car with one hand. And doing it with a jack seemed like cheating."

Mom's eyebrows draw together. Yikes! I hoped she wouldn't hear about me using the jack. *Boulder, you're not helping!*

But he's not done. "But he came up with a great idea when I couldn't hold that rock. He reminded me to dig deep." Boulder smiles at me. "If you feel Super, you'll be Super."

I nod. I *did* feel Super when I realized I knew how to save the day, even without a superpower.

"Thanks for helping me steer the rock where it couldn't hurt anyone." Boulder holds his hand out to me. I take it and try not to flinch as he grips mine too hard.

Mom blinks and looks like she's taking this in. But I can tell she's not fully convinced.

Then Thorn steps forward. "I agree, Principal Champion. There was no one here with the right power to stop that rock. We didn't see it from the greenhouse until it was way too late."

The vine in Thorn's hair loops up and grips my wrist in thanks.

"Thanks for saving my bot," I whisper in return.

As if to confirm that there was no Super here who could fix the situation, Mrs. Iceberg finally ambles around the maze, taking in the situation with wide, ocean-blue eyes.

Mom's stern expression softens. "Well, I guess you're right, Cole. I'm glad you have friends here who see the value of your science knowledge even when I'm slow to."

She wraps me in a big, mushy hug right there in front of everyone. It's the second-biggest offense after using my mortifying middle name. But I did almost die from being crushed by a boulder, so I wrap my arms around Mom's waist and hug her back, for a second.

Then I let out a groan. "I'm okay, I'm okay, Mom. Let go."

"All right, everyone." She turns to the crowd. "Time to get back to class."

"Science students, I think we've had enough energy excitement for today," Mr. Slumber says. "We'll pick this experiment back up tomorrow."

As the crowd disperses, Thorn comes over and gives me a hug. One more tingly and less monumentally embarrassing than Mom's. "Seriously, Cole, thanks for saving everyone in the greenhouse. Sometimes it feels like we're the 'least-Super' Supers. People are always forgetting plant powers when they're trying to figure out how to save the day. I'm really glad you didn't forget about us."

My cheeks flame to a zillion degrees, and I search for something to say, but fail completely.

Boulder saves me by butting in. "Thanks for covering me back there, Cole. You've got skill. I'm gonna make you my sidekick so you can use levers and energy and whatever to make my super strength extra super."

That's Boulder. Even after I save the day, he finds a way to make it all about him.

"Thanks, Boulder," I say. "But you know, since I saved the maze, the greenhouse, and all the Supers in them, maybe you should be *my* sidekick."

Sidekick lets out an indignant beep.

"You're right. I already have a sidekick," I say. "So you'll have to be my bot's sidekick, Boulder."

Boulder laughs out loud like that's the funniest thing he's ever heard. He slaps me on the shoulder so hard I almost face-plant into the dirt. "Good one, Cole."

"And your first duty as Sidekick's sidekick," I tell Boulder, "is to carry him around school for the rest of the day. He took a bad jolt when Thorn and

her vine rescued him from the boulder. One of his wheels is bent out of alignment."

As if to demonstrate, Sidekick moves forward, whirring every time the dented part of his wheel hits the ground.

Boulder picks Sidekick up and gives the bot's metal head a noogie. "You'll be okay, little buddy," he says as the four of us—Boulder, Thorn, Sidekick, and me—head back to the front doors of HERO Junior High together.

The Superhero Alliance flag above the building waves as if congratulating me on a job well done. For the first time, I feel like I belong at this school. Like I'm one of the few and the powerful who can save humankind from peril.

I send Mireya a quick text. *Can you meet me at your mom's garage this afternoon? Sidekick needs some first aid.*

She texts back immediately. *What's wrong with Sidekick?*

I smile and reply. *Have I got a story for you.*

Chapter Nine

Reassembling Sidekick

After school, I'm in Mrs. Morales's auto shop. The scent of motor oil hangs in the air. Clangs and whirs come from the other side of the shop, where mechanics are working on cars up on lifts. But Mrs. Morales is helping us. She's got Sidekick's wheel on a truing stand in front of her and is spinning it slowly, searching for all the places where it's misaligned.

Thank goodness for Mireya's mom and her

shop. I'd never be able to keep Sidekick in shape if it weren't for her.

Mireya sits beside me, passing me a bag of mixed nuts and chomping on some of her own. She wants the scoop on everything that happened today.

"I can't believe it!" she says after I finish my story. "You used STEM superpowers to save the day and I didn't even get to see it! That's so unfair!"

I laugh. "I'm the only one at HERO Junior High who thinks my STEM knowledge is super. By tomorrow, Boulder will have forgotten that *he* didn't save the day." I don't mention that the way Thorn looked at me after her near miss makes me feel warm deep in my chest.

"Remind him," Mireya tells me. "Every. Single. Day. Maybe he'll pay more attention in science class rather than causing trouble and getting Sidekick messed up."

Sidekick, who stands with his left side propped up on a spare tire, lets out a sharp trill of agreement.

"Here's where your problem is," Mrs. Morales says. She starts tightening one of the spokes to pull the wheel into shape. "We'll have you back on two wheels in no time."

"Thank you, Mrs. Morales," I say.

"Boulder's so lucky you were there," Mireya continues. "And so am I. What if your mom kicked him out of HERO Junior High and he ended up at Middletown with me? A Super with no sense wouldn't just threaten a couple classes of kids. He might destroy the whole school. And imagine how much trouble he could get into on a field trip to the science center or the zoo."

I laugh at Mireya's horrified expression. But she's not wrong. "Yeah, well, now he's Sidekick's sidekick, so we'll be in charge of keeping him out of trouble."

"Good luck with that!" she says.

I smile at my human and bot best friends. Yeah, keeping an eye on Boulder will take some work. I have a feeling I'll need to use my knowledge again when he overdoes another workout trying to outdo Bolt or bulk up as much as Captain Republic. I'm not sure how I'll save the day next time.

But somehow, I don't mind. Maybe that's part of feeling like I belong at HERO Junior High. I have friends now. Keeping an eye on them should be part of my job.

That's what it means to be a STEM superhero.

Superpower Spotlight

Super Strength

In 2020, an Icelander achieved the heaviest dead lift ever. He lifted 1,104.5 pounds (501 kg) to hip level. At the time, he weighed 425 pounds (193 kg). This means he lifted approximately 2.6 times his own body weight. This is an incredible feat.

However, many insects can do so much more. For example, some beetles can lift 100 times their body weight. Different ants can lift 10 to 50 times their body weight. One reason for this strength is the insects' small sizes.

For example, ants have light bodies. They also wear their skeletons on the outside. So, an ant's muscles do not have to provide much support to the skeleton. All the muscles' strength can go toward lifting other objects. On the other hand, humans must carry their own body weight. Muscles have less strength left over to carry other things.

Also, many insects have simpler body systems. Important body processes such as breathing and blood flow take less energy. So, insects can put more energy toward building strong outside skeletons. These skeletons carry the insects' weight.

People have started following insects' examples.

They have created exoskeletons. Users wear these robotic suits. The suits allow users to carry heavy loads. For example, an item that is 200 pounds (91 kg) might feel like it is only 10 pounds (4.5 kg) to the user. Users can easily do hours of hard work that they would normally soon tire from. The suits also protect users from getting hurt doing hard tasks. Through a STEM solution, normal people can achieve super strength.

About the Author

Rebecca J. Allen writes middle grade stories that blend mystery and adventure and young adult stories with kick-butt heroines. Her middle grade mysteries *Showtime Sabotage* and *Math Test Mischief* were published under the pseudonym Verity Weaver. When not writing, she loves to Rollerblade, hike, practice Pilates, or attempt to reclaim her garden from encroaching weeds.

About the Illustrator

Courtney Huddleston lives in Houston, Texas, with his wife, two daughters, and two cats named Lilo and Stitch. When he's not in his home studio working, he can usually be found playing video games, drooling over the work of other artists, going on long walks, or playing pranks on the family. While he gets inspiration from everything around him, his favorite way to get inspired is through travel. Courtney has been to most of the states in the United States, and he has visited more than a dozen other countries. He is currently searching for less-expensive inspirations.

Take a sneak peek at an excerpt from
Cole Champion Takes On the Villains,
another story from HERO Junior High.

Before I started at HERO Junior High, I only knew one Super: Mom. I never expected to get closer to Captain Republic than watching commercials where he tells me that Super Fruity O's are part of a nutritious breakfast. I know nothing about villains. What makes someone my age choose the dark side over being a future hero?

"What power do you think Pink has?" I ask in a low voice. The girl's curly blond hair is streaked with pink and pulled into pigtails. She blows a huge bubble, letting it pop loudly. She looks ready to shoot an ad for bubble gum or lip gloss, not represent WICKED Junior High in today's Challenge.

"World's largest gum bubble?" Bolt says with a snort. "But the guy behind her—he looks dangerous."

I want to disagree, but I can't. He's wearing a blood-colored super suit patterned like brains, and his eyebrows are drawn down in an expression of sharp annoyance. He holds his hands to his chest, tapping his fingertips together as if he's scheming up some master plan to win today's Challenge. Or maybe take over the world.

"I get a bad feeling from that girl in the gray super suit." Thorn shivers. "Like she'd use her power to negate mine—to take away the sun. She must be a storm power."

The girl's suit is patterned with wind gusts, and her hair swirls like it's caught in a breeze that affects no one but her. I definitely hope the storm Super can't take away Thorn's power. I have a feeling we'll need every hero-in-training's power going at full force to beat these guys in the Challenge.

"Why is everyone so confident these future villains will keep the truce?" I ask. "They are *villains*, after all. Backstabbing comes with the territory."

"There are no guarantees. I recommend constant vigilance." Boulder puffs out his chest.

I'm suddenly worried that Mom might be right to be concerned about my safety today. "How many end up transferring to HERO Junior High after a Challenge?" Hopefully, most will be convinced to defend humankind.

"None," Bolt says, her eyes narrowing.

I blink a couple times as I take that in. "But I thought turning potential villains to the heroes' side was the point of the Challenge."

Boulder waves his hand dismissively. "That's what the teachers say, but the real reason is to size up WICKED Junior High's students so the Alliance can prepare to defeat them."

WHAT HAPPENS NEXT?

FIND OUT IN:

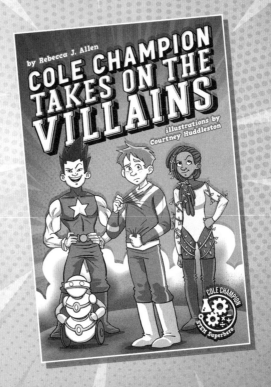

When the students at **HERO Junior High** compete against another school's villains-in-training, Cole Champion is the only one who thinks the villains are acting suspicious. Can he get his super friends to work together in time to defeat the villains?